Learning to Read, Step by Step!

Ready to Read   Preschool–Kindergarten
• big type and easy words • rhyme and rhythm • picture clues
For children who know the alphabet and are eager to
begin reading.

Reading with Help   Preschool–Grade 1
• basic vocabulary • short sentences • simple stories
For children who recognize familiar words and sound out
new words with help.

Reading on Your Own   Grades 1–3
• engaging characters • easy-to-follow plots • popular topics
For children who are ready to read on their own.

Reading Paragraphs   Grades 2–3
• challenging vocabulary • short paragraphs • exciting stories
For newly independent readers who read simple sentences
with confidence.

Ready for Chapters   Grades 2–4
• chapters • longer paragraphs • full-color art
For children who want to take the plunge into chapter books
but still like colorful pictures.

STEP INTO READING® is designed to give every child a successful
reading experience. The grade levels are only guides; children will progress
through the steps at their own speed, developing confidence in their reading.
Remember, a lifetime love of reading starts with a single step!

*This book is dedicated to
all the big people who are
helping smaller people
learn to read.
The StoryBots love you!*

Designed by Greg Mako

All rights reserved. Published in the United States by Random House Children's Books, a division of Penguin Random House LLC, 1745 Broadway, New York, NY 10019, and in Canada by Penguin Random House Canada Limited, Toronto.

Step into Reading, Random House, and the Random House colophon are registered trademarks of Penguin Random House LLC.

StoryBots, Netflix, and all related titles, logos, and characters are trademarks of Netflix, Inc.

Visit us on the Web!
StepIntoReading.com
rhcbooks.com

Educators and librarians, for a variety of teaching tools, visit us at RHTeachersLibrarians.com

ISBN 978-0-593-38049-9 (trade) — ISBN 978-0-593-38050-5 (lib. bdg.) — ISBN 978-0-593-38051-2 (ebook)

Printed in the United States of America

10 9 8 7 6 5 4 3 2 1

STORYBOTS®

THE BEST
CHRISTMAS GIFT!

by Scott Emmons

illustrated by Nikolas Ilic

Random House 🏠 New York

The StoryBots
are full of cheer.

They love this
merry time of year!

The holidays
bring many joys
and lots of gifts
for girls and boys.

Santa bring

in his sleigh

before we wake

on Christmas Day.

A gift can come
from others, too,
like moms and dads—
and kids like you!

Great gifts can be
a model train,
a stuffed giraffe,
or else a plane!

Which gift is best?

What could it be?

Is it a pair of skates
or a new TV?

Or could it be
a dinosaur
that roars and crawls
across the floor?

"My goodness!
Now I see," says Bo.
"Which gift is best?
At last I know!

"It is not any
kind of toy
that brings us all
the greatest joy!"

The greatest gift

is what we share,

like smiles and hugs,
which show we care.

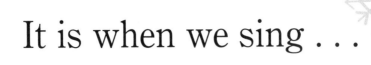

It is when we sing . . .

. . . or share a ride!

With friends, we feel
so good inside!

The greatest gift
is not a game
or a talking doll
that says her name.

It is not a skateboard
or a baseball glove.

It is the time we spend
with the ones we love!
Merry Christmas!